Brenda Berman, Wedding Expert

Brenda Berman, Wedding Expert

by Jane Breskin Zalben

Illustrated by Victoria Chess

Clarion Books • New York

Clarion Books
an imprint of Houghton Mifflin Harcourt Publishing Company
215 Park Avenue South, New York, NY 10003
Text copyright © 2009 by Jane Breskin Zalben
Illustrations © 2009 by Victoria Chess

The illustrations were executed in watercolor.
The text was set in 13-point Tiffany.

www.clarionbooks.com

Manufactured in China

Library of Congress Cataloging-in-Publication Data
Zalben, Jane Breskin.
Brenda Berman, wedding expert / by Jane Breskin Zalben ; illustrated by Victoria Chess.
p. cm.
Summary: When Brenda's favorite uncle decides to marry, Brenda sees visions of a gold
lamé flower-girl's outfit, until Uncle Harry and his bride-to-be show up with her niece.
Includes cake recipe.

ISBN: 978-0-618-31321-1

[1. Weddings—Fiction. 2. Flower girls—Fiction. 3. Uncles—Fiction.
4. Friendship—Fiction.] I. Chess, Victoria, ill. II. Title.

PZ7.Z254Br 2009
[Fic]—dc22

2006034851

WKT   10 9 8 7 6 5 4 3 2 1

In memory of Aunt Carol, who eloped with Uncle Morty,
robbing me of my dreams of a gold lamé flower-girl dress,
to Joann Hill, who unlocked those dreams with her wedding plans,

— AND —

most of all with love to my son, Alexander,
on his marriage to Marni.
— J.B.Z.

For Ayat, and *her* dreams
— V.C.

Contents

1
The Big News

At seven thirty-three Sunday morning, Brenda was standing on the fluffy toilet seat cover, counting her freckles one by one in the bathroom mirror, when her mother let out a scream. "Uncle Harry's getting married!" she yelled louder than a crowd at midnight on New Year's Eve. "To that sweet, sweet Florrie he's been seeing."

"So your baby brother's finally tying the knot!" Papa shouted back.

Uncle Harry was Brenda's favorite uncle in the whole wide world. Ever since she was born, she'd had him all to herself—except for her brother, Max, but that didn't count, since Brenda was older and *always* got her way.

She ran down the hall into Max's bedroom. "Did you hear the big news?"

"Like I could sleep through it." Max rubbed his eyes.

"You know how Uncle Harry takes us to amusement parks and doesn't care how many times we repeat the rides?" said Brenda. "And how he teaches us magic tricks,

making rabbits appear and *you* disappear? And how he comes over to baby-sit and reads us stories way past midnight? Well, from now on, for the rest of our lives, it's going to be 'Uncle Harry *and* Aunt Florrie.'"

"Come up for some air, Brenda." Max yawned. "Florrie's okay."

"Will she be okay when she doesn't let us go on the roller coaster five times in a row? Will she be okay when she doesn't let us eat hot dogs with 'the works' for breakfast?

Will she be okay when she makes us go to bed so early that we don't get to hear even one story?"

"Florrie would do that?" Max was wide awake now. "And Uncle Harry is marrying her? What a traitor!"

"Exactly." Brenda gave Max a smug smile.

Brenda's world was caving in all around her. She thought it couldn't get any worse. But then it did.

Brenda overheard Mama say to Papa, "Won't Max look cute as a button as the ring bearer? And Brenda and Lucy absolutely adorable as flower girls, together in taffeta? Florrie's thinking: *Everything* lavender." Three words hung in the air like bees buzzing: *Taffeta. Lavender.* And *Lucy.*

Ever since Brenda was five years old, she had dreamed of wearing a gold lamé flower-girl dress with sparkly shoes, like ballet slippers, and a shiny diamond tiara in her hair. She'd walk down the aisle—*alone*—before the bride and groom, sprinkling pale pink rose petals on the path to the altar. She'd wear her mother's expensive perfume, eat tiny hors d'oeuvres with names she couldn't even pronounce, and stay up extra late. Brenda had this whole wedding planned, and it wasn't really important whose wedding it was.

But now she was going to lose Uncle Harry without even getting gold lamé to make it better. She'd be wearing ugly, slippery lavender taffeta. In the space of less than an hour, Uncle Harry had gone from being her favorite uncle in the entire world to the worst uncle on the planet.

Brenda gave Max a devilish grin. "Bet the ring bearer wears lavender, too."

"In your dreams," he protested, waving a toy rubber sword in the air.

The only thing Max was probably good for was carrying the ring. But Max was such a klutz, he'd definitely trip and mess everything up—a thought that made Brenda smile inside. Which led her to the next problem. *Who's this Lucy?*

2
Florrie Says "Sorry"

That evening, Mama's three sisters fussed about while Mama and Papa put finishing touches on a sign hanging across the living room: CONGRATULATIONS HARRY AND FLO! When Harry and Florrie arrived, blue glitter from the sign sprinkled onto Uncle Harry's head as he cheerfully picked up Max, the way he always did. Their brand-new aunt-to-be made kissing sounds at all of them, smacking her lips. Brenda wanted to barf.

"How are my favorite niece and nephew in the whole wide world?" Uncle Harry asked.

Before Brenda could answer, Florrie gave Harry a look, then motioned in the direction of a girl Brenda's age who was edging between them. Brenda saw that look.

"This is Florrie's niece, Lucy. We're baby-sitting." Uncle Harry cleared his throat and patted Lucy's wildly curly hair. Brenda patted her own, which was like strands of spaghetti. She hated Lucy on sight. "How are two of my three favorite children," he corrected himself, "in the whole wide world?"

Brenda thought, *He's acting like Lucy's a niece too!*

The way he always did, Max put his arms around Uncle Harry's neck. He said in a friendly voice, "Hi, Lucy. How's it going?" as if they had known each other from the cradle.

Brenda glared at Max and muttered, "There are many traitors in this room."

She flinched when Uncle Harry tried to kiss her on the cheek, and stepped back when Florrie nearly squashed her with a hug, going toward her forehead with her bright red lips. Now that Florrie had robbed Brenda of her special wedding plans, Brenda simply couldn't look her in the eye. And just as she had plans, so did all her aunts—Uncle Harry's older sisters.

"Remember when you got married, Iris?" Aunt Zelda reminisced. "And it snowed so hard, the entire family had a sleepover in the banquet hall?"

"How could I forget the Blizzard of Brooklyn?" groaned Aunt Iris. "Cousin Norman snored in my ear all night. So we'll make it a summer wedding."

"A summer wedding?" Aunt Matilda turned to Aunt Zelda. "Remember when you got married? It was so hot, the ice sculpture on the dessert table melted. Talk about

an ice cream float! I should have worn my bathing suit and goggles instead of a gown."

"Ah, yes, the Famous Flood of Flushing," Aunt Zelda sighed. "So we'll make it a big fall wedding."

"An autumn wedding? Why wait so long?" asked Mama. "Spring is nice."

"I was kind of thinking of a small June wedding," whispered Florrie. "Just the immediate family and a few close friends."

No one seemed to hear her except Brenda. *Maybe she'll see how I feel now,* thought Brenda. *Being ignored.*

Florrie turned toward Mama. "And what about yours?"

"Tell us again what happened," Brenda and Max said together.

"Well, " said Mama, "Papa rushed to the temple at the corner of Main and Hamilton, while I went to the one written on the invitation—at the corner of Main and Madison. He was waiting in one place, while I was waiting in another.

"Finally"—she rolled her eyes at Papa—"when a different bride showed up with another groom, Papa realized he might be in the wrong spot. Next time, we'll go together!"

"Next time?" Papa poked Mama in the side.

Everyone in the room began to laugh, especially Lucy.

"Well, I don't think that's funny one bit," Brenda burst out, frowning at Lucy. "Because if my mama and papa didn't find each other, then there would never have been me and my brother." And she stomped out of the room.

Florrie followed her into the kitchen. When Florrie put her hands on Brenda's shoulders, every bone in Brenda's body tensed. "I'm sorry I'm taking up your uncle's time and that you have to share him," said this stranger, who

was now going to be her aunt, "but I love him to pieces."

Tears rolled down Brenda's face. She tried to hide them, gulping between gasps.

There were three things she was certain about, and nothing would ever change her mind:

1. *I won't ever wear taffeta. (Especially any shade of purple.)*

2. *I won't ever like Lucy. (Not ever, ever, ever!)*

3. *I won't ever forgive Uncle Harry. (Or the rest of my family for going along with him on this crazy idea.)*

"And I'm not wearing *anything* lavender!" shouted Brenda. "Not even a purple bow!"

Florrie continued calmly, "Maybe we could go to Fabric Circus together? I need to choose crinoline for a veil. I would love your help. And you could pick out cloth too—for a dress to make."

Had Brenda heard right? "O-okay," she stammered. "I'm thinking gold lamé."

"Gold lamé?" Florrie's voice raised a whole octave.

"Yeah," Brenda repeated with attitude, "gold lamé."

Florrie put her arm around Brenda reassuringly. "You'll look like a princess."

Brenda didn't feel like facing her family, so she slipped into her room without saying good night. After a while, Mama tiptoed in and sat on the edge of her bed. Brenda pulled the covers up to her eyes, almost hiding them.

"Could you try to open your heart just a little?" Mama asked softly.

And she kissed Brenda right where Florrie had kissed her earlier, wiping away the faint smudge of Florrie's bright red lipstick.

"I'll try, Mama."

"That's all I ask."

As Brenda fell asleep, her mind swirled, filling again with flowers and wedding marches. *Maybe I will get my dream dress after all!*

3
An Almost Perfect Day

When Florrie picked up Brenda for their shopping spree, her precious niece, Lucy, was with her, dressed in plum tights, looking like a prune. "What is *she* doing here?" Brenda mumbled to herself. Brenda's mother had begged her to try and be nice. This was not a good beginning.

Florrie grabbed both girls' hands. "Won't this be fun?"

Brenda and Lucy remained silent the whole bus ride to the textile store as Florrie went on and on about nothing.

Brenda's eyes widened when she saw a sign in the window: SALE TODAY. SPECIAL ON CRINOLINE. When they got to the counter where tulle was displayed, the crimson fabric reminded her of the tutu she had worn in the ballet recital last winter when she played the Red Fairy. "What a veil that would make!" she shouted with glee.

"Aunt Florrie, you'd look like a clown," Lucy said.

Brenda glared at her, pouting. "It's bright and cheerful."

Florrie fingered some delicate off-white veiling. "I was

sort of thinking of a pale ecru for my bridal veil. But this is a pretty, deep shade of red."

"Like your lipstick." Brenda grinned from ear to ear.

"I'll take three yards." Florrie was trying her best to make Brenda happy, Brenda could tell.

Brenda searched everywhere for gold cloth—bolt after bolt, color after color—but no lamé. Her heart sank. Then, off in the corner where the satins and silks were, Florrie found a piece of honey-colored cloth, like eggshells from

a farm. There was just enough for one dress. Brenda bit her lower lip to keep from shouting for joy. *Enough for me! None for Lucy.* Maybe this would mean Lucy couldn't be a flower girl now, since she wouldn't have the same dress.

Lucy looked as if Brenda had eaten the last spoonful of chocolate cream pie without asking her if she wanted a bite. "What about *me?*" she asked.

"Oh, I'm sure you have your own ideas." Florrie led the girls to another table, and wrapped Lucy in yards of lavender. Twirling around in front of a mirror, wrapped in taffeta from head to toe, Lucy looked like a lilac bush.

"Won't it look weird?" asked Brenda. "Us going down the aisle not dressed alike?"

"But you're not alike." Florrie leaned over and looked into Brenda's eyes. "You're *very* different people."

Brenda glanced at Lucy, who was beaming, and then back at Florrie.

"Brenda, I think your plan of not having matching flower-girl outfits is perfect." Florrie went on. "And Max can wear whatever he wants."

"Even if it's his warrior space outfit from a galactic empire?" Brenda asked.

"What people wear isn't what weddings are about, is it? They're about love."

Florrie gave her a kiss on the top of her head. Brenda let out a deep sigh, noticing that Lucy didn't look too happy about that kiss. *Maybe Lucy is bent out of shape about losing her aunt—the way I am about losing my uncle.*

Florrie chose tiny pearl buttons to sew up the backs of all three dresses. "This way our dresses will have something that matches," she said. Brenda thought pearls were a bit too fussy, but she decided to keep her mouth shut this once.

It had been an almost-perfect day, even if Brenda's dress wasn't going to be pure gold lamé. That night, she dreamed of the silk, shimmering and shining and rippling in the sunlight like waves in the ocean.

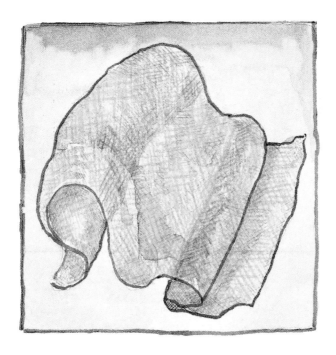

4
Honeymoon in Hawaii

Sometimes, just when everything seems to be going along okay, *something happens.* A couple of weeks before the big event, when Brenda waltzed into the family room, she found Mama standing there sniffling. "Harry and Florrie eloped last night!" she announced. "We got a call from Hawaii. They thought it would make life easier on everyone."

Brenda stopped dead in her tracks. "They *what?*"

"Got hitched in Honolulu," said Papa. "Zelda, Iris, and Matilda are going to give him grief big-time when he gets back. They were really looking forward to a bash!"

"*They* were really looking forward?" Brenda blurted out. "What about *me?*"

"Be happy for him," Papa said consolingly. "So we won't have some fancy-schmancy wedding. Who cares?"

"*I* care." Brenda was beyond disappointed. No big wedding? No ceremony? No flower-girl outfit? Harry and Florrie had now robbed her of her happiness not once but twice. "I'm never, ever going to speak to them again for as long as I live."

"Trust me, Brenda, Drama Queen, you will," said Papa, rolling his eyes.

Two weeks later—the longest two weeks of Brenda's entire life—the newlyweds came back. They picked up Lucy along the way to Brenda's house. All three were wearing matching T-shirts that said "Maui Wowie," and they had orchid leis around their necks. Harry and Florrie placed their flowers around Mama and Papa's necks. Naturally, Lucy kept hers.

They gave Brenda turquoise flip-flops, which she wouldn't

put on. Lucy was already wearing zebra-striped ones. And
Max got polka-dot sunglasses, which he wouldn't take off.
"You think you're cool," Brenda said snidely to Max, "but you
look like a doofus."

Lucy laughed like she was Brenda's best friend, which
she wasn't. And that made Brenda even madder.

Brenda put her hands over her ears while Aunt Florrie
told about falling off a donkey on a volcano trail. She whistled
while Uncle Harry sang and Aunt Florrie did the hula with
hand motions. To make matters worse, everyone joined in

dancing, except Brenda. Afterward, Brenda refused to look at pictures of their honeymoon. All that lovey-dovey stuff was even grosser than the dancing.

Mama shot Brenda a stern look that said, *Brenda Berman, enough is enough!*

Brenda thought, *Just because everyone else is so happy, why do I have to act cheerful too?*

Brenda stared at Lucy, who was picking at the flower garland around her neck and watching her favorite aunt smooch all over Uncle Harry. But when Florrie gave Max a big hug, Lucy didn't look too happy. As Lucy headed to the table to get a tropical drink Mama had put in the punchbowl for the occasion, Brenda seized the moment. "You know, I already had a pattern picked out for my dress."

"Me too," admitted Lucy.

"And big plans for the wedding."

"Me too," repeated Lucy.

"Come on." Brenda pulled Lucy into the downstairs bathroom and locked the door. "Are you as mad at them as I am?"

"Madder. I've wanted to be a flower girl my whole life."

"Me too!" Brenda screeched at the top of her lungs.

This was even better than Brenda had hoped for. She lowered her voice to a top-secret level. "So let's give them a wedding. The kind *we* want. After all, we're cousins." She had just realized this.

"Hey, we are, aren't we?" Lucy smiled for the first time.

"We could make lanterns," suggested Brenda.

"With paper chains," added Lucy.

"And a wedding cake. Piled high with plenty of frosting," Brenda chimed in. "Mama's recipes are the best."

They walked back into the family room together, holding hands. "I was thinking," Brenda said out loud.

Lucy coughed.

"*We* were thinking," Brenda corrected herself, "that *both* nieces"—it was the first time Brenda had used the word "niece," acting as if Florrie was family, which, let's face it, she was—"could make you two a *real* wedding."

Aunt Florrie's face turned bright red, like her lipstick. Speechless, she looked at Uncle Harry, who was speechless too.

Max, who knew how bossy Brenda could get, broke in, grimacing. "My sister, Brenda Berman, is *the* expert on everything. Are you sure you want her help?"

"Well, I guess that means she'll make a perfect wedding planner, then," Mama answered.

Brenda narrowed her eyes at Max as everyone else laughed out loud.

"Who in their right minds could pass up a Brenda Berman event?" asked Uncle Harry.

"Not me. I'm in," said Aunt Florrie.

"Me too!" the aunts all cheered.

"Sounds like we're having a wedding!" cried Mama and Papa.

Lucy slept over. They could hardly go to sleep that night because they were making plans.

Before the big day arrived, everyone made paper chains and lanterns. Brenda and Lucy picked wildflowers and made a wreath for Aunt Florrie to wear with her veil. Max eyed the drooping petals. "Looks like weeds." Brenda

ignored him and prayed they would stay fresh. She thought
it was better than a tiara or a crown. And so did Lucy.

"It's gorgeous!" Mama beamed. "You're both born artists."

Brenda and Lucy felt very proud.

5

Brenda Berman, Wedding Expert

There's nothing like an outdoor June wedding if it's a gloriously sunny day. But if there's a storm with hail the size of golf balls, it's a total disaster. And that's exactly what occurred the day of the backyard party.

Lucy was in tears. So was Brenda.

"My life is ruined!" Brenda wailed.

Wearing her "I-want-to-disappear-off-the-face-of-the-earth-and-forget-this-ever-happened" expression, Brenda went to her room and put a sign on the door: DO NOT ENTER! EVEN IN CASE OF EMERGENCY! While Max ran around the house squealing at this wondrous summer sight—frozen flowerbeds and trees stiff as peanut brittle—Brenda lay on her bed like a limp fish.

Moments later, there was a gentle knock. "Your father is raking hail," Aunt Florrie said through the keyhole. "Your mother is blow-drying centerpieces. And I ordered the sun," she said, as the first few rays peeked through Brenda's window, "because I love your uncle to pieces."

Brenda got up, unlocked the door and opened it just a crack.

"I have a surprise for you." Aunt Florrie put a piece of icy hail in Brenda's sweaty palm. "I don't have diamonds, but I have you, and that's better than all the diamonds in the whole wide world. When I was getting your uncle, I didn't know that you came with the package." She handed Brenda something wrapped in shiny gold tissue paper. Brenda untied the ribbon as Lucy came racing up the stairs.

"*For me?*" Brenda caught her breath when she saw the shimmer of honey silk as the sun came out.

"Even though there isn't going to be a big wedding, every person should have a special outfit," said Aunt Florrie, "because life is full of occasions that should be celebrated."

"Even if it's not gold lamé," chimed in Lucy, spinning in a lavender taffeta dress.

"You *made* them for us?" Brenda could hardly believe it. "When did you have the time?"

"It's the least I could do," Aunt Florrie said.

Both girls hugged her.

Brenda put on her party dress and skipped downstairs into the wet backyard.

It was full of guests. Happy. And smiling.

Papa played the violin. Brenda and Lucy sprinkled rose petals. Max followed with the ring perched on a pillow that Florrie had sewn from the leftover fabrics. He almost slipped on a soggy patch of grass but saved himself just in time. Then Mama and her older sisters walked Uncle Harry under a tall branch of the willow tree, which got so crowded underneath that there wasn't room for the whole family. All the sisters were wearing matching Hawaiian muumuus to go with Brenda and Lucy's theme of "The Big Island."

Everyone turned around to wait for the bride. Brenda got a lump in her throat when she saw her aunt walking across the lawn wearing the wilting wreath and crimson veil. Aunt Florrie joined them under the willow.

She told Uncle Harry, "I will always love you to pieces."

Uncle Harry lifted her veil. "I will always love you to pieces too," he said.

They kissed. Papa, Mama, and her sisters wiped tears from their eyes. Everyone clapped, sang out "Mazel tov! Good luck," and danced around them in a circle.

And this time, when the party got under way and Aunt Florrie did the hula, Brenda stood alongside her, trying to learn the movements, copying each and every step. And so did Lucy, right beside her cousin Brenda.

As the sun began to set, Papa lit tiki torches. Flames glowed wildly around the luau feast. Family and friends raised cups of Brenda's Passion Punch as Uncle Harry gave a toast. "This was the most perfect wedding party!"

"And it's not over!" shouted Brenda, Lucy, and Max.

They led Harry and Florrie to a corner in the backyard next to a plastic palm tree lit with colored lights. Under an awning was a poster: WELCOME TO WAIKIKI! Lucy handed each of them a necklace of dandelions strung on yarn. With tears in her eyes, Florrie took off her sandals and dipped her toes into a plastic wading pool surrounded by shells and sand that Max had emptied from his ant farm earlier that day. "Hope the ants are gone!" Max whispered to Brenda, spelling out "A-N-T-S," not "A-U-N-T-S."

"What can we say?" Uncle Harry sighed, settling into a lawn chair. "It doesn't get much better than this."

Aunt Florrie agreed, sipping a smoothie as she sat by his side.

"Yes, it does," Brenda said with an apologetic grin. "Sorry, Aunt Florrie, that you wore a red veil instead of the one you wanted. Sorry you had a wreath with dead flowers. And sorry I was Brenda the Brute." She threw her arms around her aunt's neck. "I love you to pieces."

"I love you too," said Aunt Florrie as she hugged Brenda.

Lucy put her arms around Uncle Harry. "Thanks for letting me be a flower girl at your wedding. I got my dream wish."

"Oh!" Uncle Harry cocked his head to one side. "And I got mine."

"I'm glad you're my new uncle," she said.

"And I'm glad you're my new niece." He looked past her and winked at Brenda.

And this time, Brenda didn't mind.

After the guests had gone home, Mama, Papa, Max, Brenda, and Lucy camped out under the stars. Uncle Harry slept soundly in a hammock nearby. Aunt Florrie, well . . . not so soundly. Uncle Harry yawned like a hippo, then snored like a bulldog. But Aunt Florrie loved him to pieces, anyway. And so did the rest of the family. Especially Brenda. More than the whole wide world.

Mama's Famous Wedding Cake

The cake came out lopsided after Max got his paws on it (and tasted the bottom layer), but Brenda and Lucy put their hearts into every stir of the spoon, so in the end who cares? It was delicious.

Children should not try making this recipe without a grownup.

3 cups sifted bleached flour
1 teaspoon baking soda
1 teaspoon baking powder
3 extra large eggs, separated
1 cup granulated sugar
$\frac{1}{4}$ cup vegetable oil
Juice of one lemon
1 cup of honey

1 cup strong coffee
1 teaspoon maple syrup
1 teaspoon powdered ginger
1 teaspoon ground cinnamon
1 teaspoon ground allspice
1 teaspoon cream of tartar
1 tablespoon grated almonds (optional)

1. Preheat oven to 350 degrees.
2. In a large bowl, sift together flour, baking soda, and baking powder.
3. In another large bowl, beat egg yolks and sugar until foamy.
4. Add oil, lemon juice, honey, coffee, and maple syrup. Mix.
5. In a separate bowl, beat egg whites with cream of tartar until stiff peaks form. (Make sure bowl and beaters are clean or stiff peaks won't form.)
6. Fold egg whites into batter with a spatula. Add grated almonds, folding gently.
7. Grease two 9-inch round layer pans that are $1\frac{1}{2}$ inches deep and one 10-inch round layer pan that is $1\frac{1}{2}$ inches deep.
8. Pour batter into pans. Pans should be two-thirds full to allow cake to double in height.

9. Bake 25 to 30 minutes. (Test with toothpick; if toothpick is dry when removed, cake is done.) Cool to room temperature before removing from pans.

Yield: 3 round layers

Note: You can use various-sized pans to make a tower effect for the wedding cake. Each layer can even be a different kind of cake—strawberry shortcake, lemon, poppy, carrot, chocolate . . . whatever you choose. Brenda's favorite is honey for her sweet Uncle Harry, the best uncle in the whole wide world. You can leave out the grated almonds if anyone is allergic to nuts.

Coconut-Vanilla-Raisin Frosting

This is Lucy's favorite tropical icing. You can use your own favorite recipe, of course!

8 ounces softened cream cheese
1 stick unsalted butter, softened to room temperature
1 pound confectioners' sugar, sifted
2 teaspoons vanilla extract
$\frac{1}{2}$ cup dark or light raisins
$\frac{1}{2}$ cup toasted pecans, chopped fine (optional)
$\frac{1}{2}$ cup coconut flakes

1. In a large bowl, blend cream cheese and butter with an electric mixer.
2. Add sugar and vanilla to mixture and blend.
3. Fold in raisins, pecans, and coconut flakes.

Yield: Enough to frost 2 or 3 stacked round layers.

Brenda's Passion Punch

The family drinks this punch year-round—not just at summer weddings!

1 liter seltzer or club soda
48 ounces cranberry juice
2 quarts grapefruit juice
1 fresh lime, for squeezing

2 fresh limes or lemons, sliced thin **by a grownup**
24 fresh raspberries (or a dozen strawberries)
3–4 trays of ice cubes (whole or crushed)
Fresh mint leaves for garnish (optional)

1. In a large punch bowl, combine seltzer with cranberry and grapefruit juices.
2. Squeeze the fresh lime and add juice to bowl. Float sliced limes (or lemons), raspberries (or strawberries), and mint leaves on top.
3. Add ice cubes.

Yield: Serves 12–14 (depending on how hot it is, and how thirsty the crowd is!)